3 8030 01642 9386
D0229497
-3 AUG 2005
-5 OCT 2005
-2 NOV 2005
14 DEC 2005
24 APR 2006
31 MAY 2006
14 JUN 2006
20 SEP 2006
-8 NOV 2006
08 DEC 2006
24 JAN 2007
25 MAR 2013
26 SEP 2014
13 APR 2015
11 MAY 2015
Tynnwyd o'r stoc
Withdrawn
CIRCULATION
DATE
LIBRARY
CAERPHILLY
COUNTY BOROUGH COUNCIL
CYNGOR BWRDEISTREF SIROL
CAERFFILI
ABERCARN LIBRARY
Please return / renew this item by the last date shown above
Dychwelwch / Adnewyddwch erbyn y dyddiad olaf y nodir yma

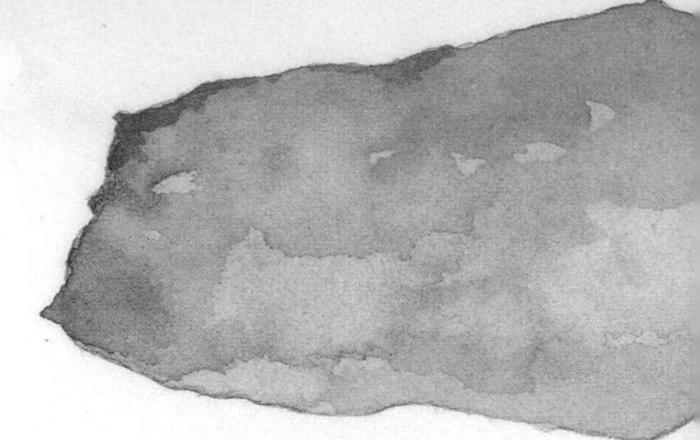

For Eleanor. A.M.
For Bebhin and Sharon, and Séana too. M-L.F.

JASMINE'S LION
A DOUBLEDAY BOOK 0385 60505 6

Published in Great Britain by Doubleday, an imprint of Random House Children's Books

This edition published 2005

1 3 5 7 9 10 8 6 4 2

Designed by Ian Butterworth

RANDOM HOUSE CHILDREN'S BOOKS
61–63 Uxbridge Road, London W5 5SA
A division of The Random House Group Ltd

RANDOM HOUSE AUSTRALIA (PTY) LTD
20 Alfred Street, Milsons Point, Sydney,
New South Wales 2061, Australia

RANDOM HOUSE NEW ZEALAND LTD
18 Poland Road, Glenfield, Auckland 10, New Zealand

RANDOM HOUSE (PTY) LTD
Endulini, 5A Jubilee Road, Parktown 2193, South Africa

THE RANDOM HOUSE GROUP Limited Reg. No. 954009
www.**kids**at**randomhouse**.co.uk

A CIP catalogue record for this book is available from the British Library.

Printed and bound in Singapore

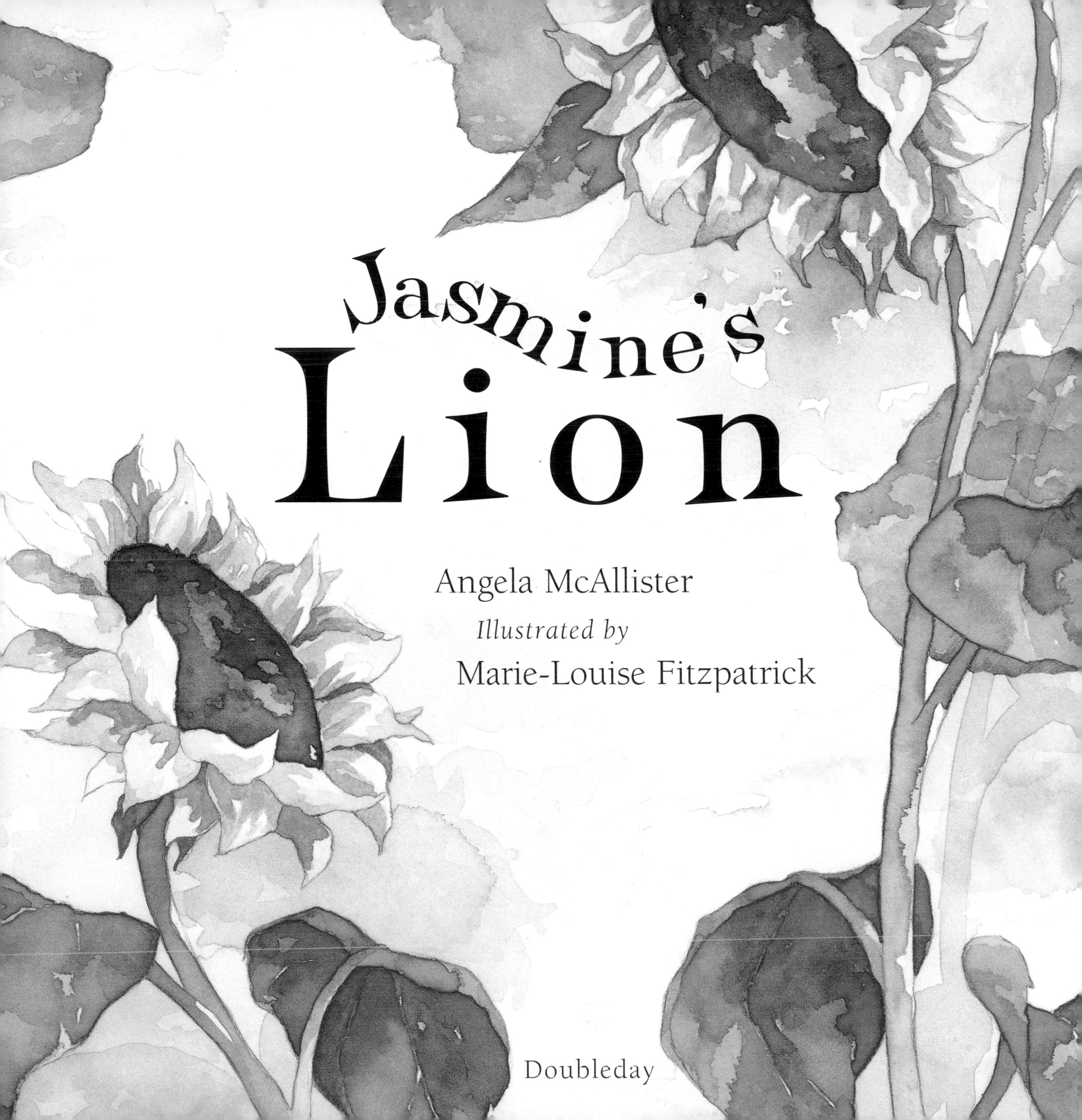

Jasmine's Lion

Angela McAllister

Illustrated by

Marie-Louise Fitzpatrick

Doubleday

One afternoon Jasmine and her mum came home from the shops. When they got to the back door Jasmine stopped.

"We can't go inside," she said. "There's a lion in the house."

"Oh dear," said Mum, "we'd better stay in the garden for a while."

"Good," said Jasmine, "I don't like playing inside."

"I know," said Mum.

Jasmine loved being in the garden.
Whether it was sunny, windy or rainy,
she always wanted to play outside.

Jasmine climbed to the top
of her climbing frame.
She imagined it was a castle.

Mum put on her gardening gloves
and pulled out some weeds.
After a while Mum said,
"Shall we go in now?"
"I'll just have a look,"
said Jasmine.

She peeped through the keyhole.
The lion was having a tea party
with all her toys.
"No, we can't go in yet," she said.

Jasmine played in the sandpit.
She imagined it was a desert. Mum
was clearing leaves from the pond
when the postman came to the gate.
"You'd better give the letters to me,
because there's a lion in the house,"
explained Jasmine.
"Yes, of course," said the postman
with a smile.

After a while Mum said,
"Shall we go in now?"
"I'll just have a look," said Jasmine.

There was a big flowerpot
under the window.
Jasmine climbed up.
The lion had been playing
with her playdough and now
he was painting big pictures.

"We can't go in yet,"
said Jasmine.

While Mum picked some apples, Jasmine crawled through the long grass. She imagined she was a tiger in the jungle.

Then Mum gave her a ride in the wheelbarrow. After a while they felt hungry.

"I think it's tea time. Shall we go in now?" said Mum.
"I'll just have a look," said Jasmine.

She pushed open the cat-flap
and peeped inside.
The lion was making
chocolate chip cookies and
the table was laid for one.

"We can't go in yet,"
said Jasmine.

Mum looked at the basket of apples. "Let's have a picnic," she said. Jasmine fetched an old rug from the shed and Mum looked in the shopping bag. She found bananas and carrots and pasties and jam doughnuts.
"This is better than inside tea," said Jasmine.

But after a while the sun went behind a cloud.
Mum gave a shiver. "Shall we go in now?" she said.
"I'll just have a look," said Jasmine.

She peered into her bedroom from the tree house.
The lion had tried to put on Jasmine's pyjamas.
He was climbing into Jasmine's bed and cuddling her bears.

Jasmine knocked on the door. The lion opened it.
"We have to come in now," said Jasmine.
"Yes, I must go," sighed the lion. "I'm afraid I can't stay here because these pyjamas are too small."
And he took them off, licked the chocolate from his whiskers and went home.

When Jasmine climbed into bed that night she found some cookie crumbs on her pillow.

"I think I'll play inside tomorrow," she told Mum as she kissed her goodnight, "just in case . . ." Jasmine yawned and hugged her bears tight. "We could get a visit from a *tiger*. . ."